How to Catch a Dragon

From the *New York Times*
Bestselling Author and Illustrator

Adam Wallace &
Andy Elkerton

sourcebooks
wonderland

Mom's cooking in the kitchen,
and Grandma's standing near.
We're getting ready for New Year's,
my favorite day all year!

奶奶

"I think we might be missing something,"
I hear my mother say.
"A dragon would bring health and fortune."
A dragon! What? No WAY!!

Every year, my friends and I
help decorate the street.
We hang *Fai Chun* and red lanterns
every couple feet.

朋友

新年

But this New Year, we're on the watch
to pick up any trail.
Oh wait—is that...? I thought I saw...
It is! A real red DRAGON'S TAIL!

This dragon can control the water?
He's cooler than we thought!
We'll have to be much smarter
to get this dragon caught!

MAGICAL DRAGON SLIDE →

We won't use tacos for this dragon—
we'll try noodles and sticky rice.
The problem is he loved them so,
he came back to eat them twice!

I thought that since our dragon ate,
he'd be ready for a nap.
But even cozy Dragon Inn
couldn't cut it as a trap!

陷阱

Dragon Inn

We hoped to catch our dragon now
with this thundering beat.
We might as well have caught the wind,
but we won't admit defeat!

We cannot lose this dragon now,
not with this massive bait!
A dragon can't resist some gold.
We'll catch him—just you wait!

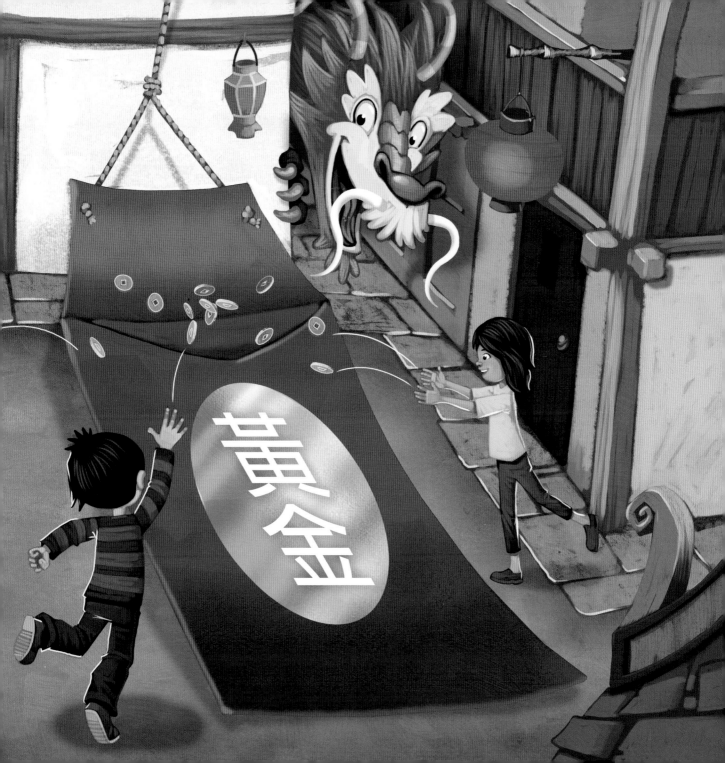

On any other day, I'd love
to catch money from the sky.
But today it means our trap fell through...
I need just one more try!

This final trap just has to work.
It is our greatest chance!
The thing that dragons love the most?
The mighty Dragon Dance!

舞龙

Our Dragon Dance is going great—
I'm having so much fun!
But where's our dragon? We've gotta catch him
before the day is done!

Oh man, we made a giant mess,
and no dragon to be seen.
That means no good health or fortune...
I guess we'd better clean.

"I'm sorry, Mom, I tried my best to make you proud this year..."

Watching fireworks with Mom
and Grandma next to me,

烟花

家庭

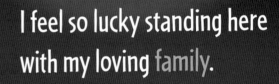

I feel so lucky standing here with my loving family.

Better luck next year!

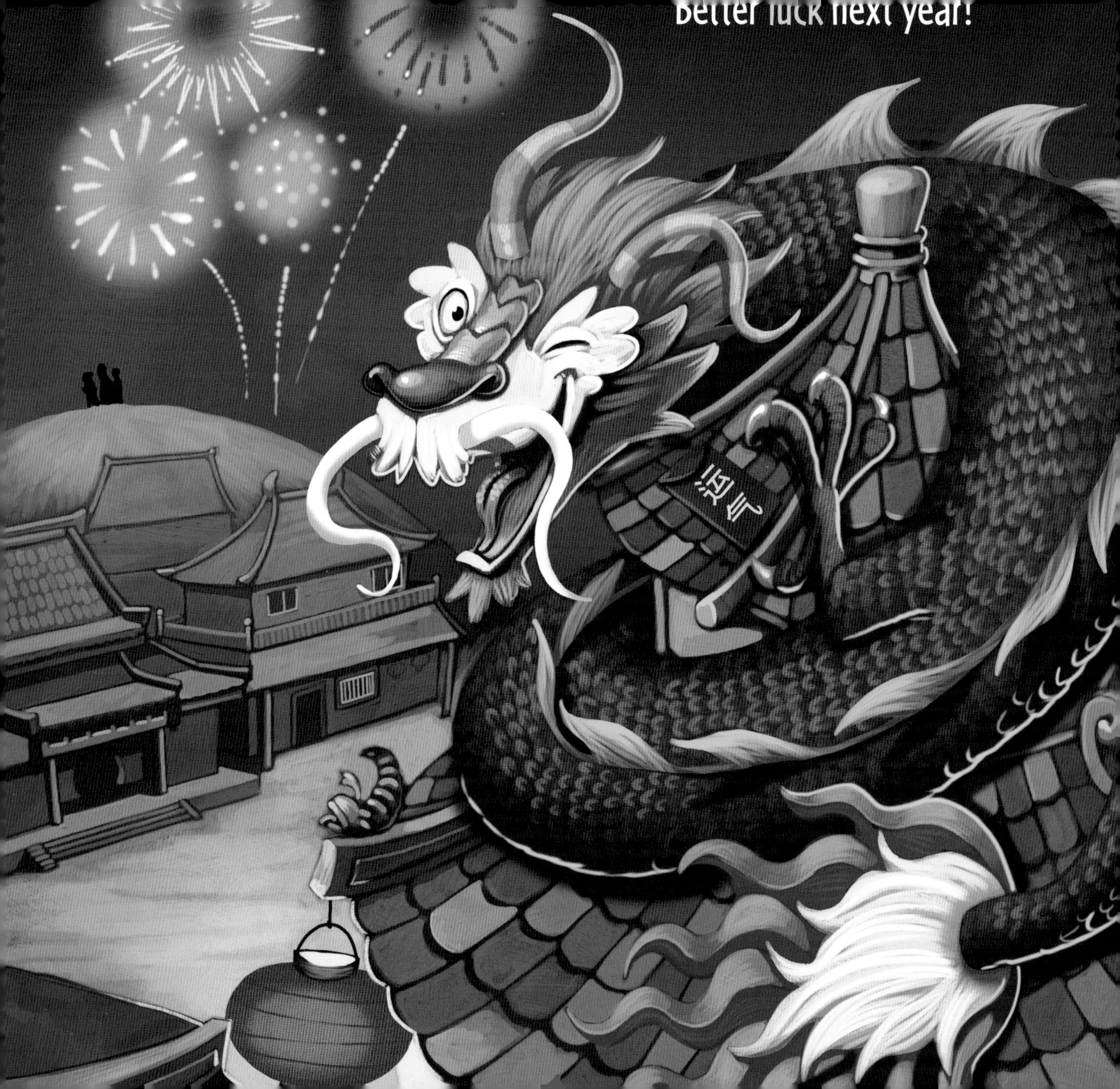

Mom's cooking in the kitchen,
and Grandma's standing near.
We're getting ready for New Year's,
my favorite day all year!

"I think we might be missing something,"
I hear my mother say.
"A dragon would bring health and fortune."
A dragon! What? No WAY!!

Every year, my friends and I
help decorate the street.
We hang *Fai Chun* and red lanterns
every couple feet.

But this New Year, we're on the watch
to pick up any trail.
Oh wait—is that? I thought I saw…
It is! A real red DRAGON'S TAIL!

This dragon can control the water?
He's cooler than we thought!
We'll have to be much smarter
to get this dragon caught!

We won't use tacos for this dragon—
we'll try noodles and sticky rice.
The problem is he loved them so,
he came back to eat them twice!

I thought that since our dragon ate,
he'd be ready for a nap.
But even cozy Dragon Inn
couldn't cut it as a trap!

We hoped to catch our dragon now
with this thundering beat.
We might as well have caught the wind,
but we won't admit defeat!

Mā ma zài chú fáng zuò fàn,
nǎi nai zhàn zài páng biān。
Wǒ men zhēng zhǔn bèi yíng xīn nián,
Shì wǒ quán nián zuì xǐ huan de yī tiān!

"Wǒ xiǎng wǒ men hǎo xiàng quē shǎo shén me。"
Wǒ tīng mǔ qīn shuō,
"Yī tiáo lóng huì dài lái jiàn kāng hé xìng yùn。"
Yī tiáo lóng! Shén me? Bù kě néng!!

Měi nián péng you hé wǒ
bāng zhù zhuāng shì jiē dào。
Měi gé jǐ yīng chǐ
wǒ men guà yī cì fēi chūn hé hóng dēng lǒng。

Dàn zhè xīn de yī nián,
wǒ men dé guān kàn yǒu hé xiàn suǒ。
ó, děng yī xià, nà shi ?wǒ xiǎng wǒ kàn dào le……。
Tā shì! Yī tiáo zhēn dí hóng sè lóng de wěi ba!

Zhè tiáo lóng néng kòng zhì shuǐ ?
Tā bǐ wǒ men xiǎng xiàng dí yào kù!
Wǒ men bì xū yào gēng cōng ming!
Cái néng bǎ zhè tiáo lóng zhuā zhù!

Wǒ men bù yòng yù mǐ juǎn gěi zhè tiáo lóng——
wǒ men huì shì yòng miàn tiáo hé nuò mǐ fàn。
Wèn tí shì tā hěn ài chī zhè xiē,
jiù huí lái chī liǎo liǎng cì!

Wǒ yǐ wéi wǒ men de lóng chī wán,
tā jiù huì xiǎng wǔ shuì。
Dàn shì shū shì lóng kè zhàn,
yě chéng bù liǎo xiàn jǐng!

Wǒ men xī wàng xiàn zài néng yòng
zhè léi míng de shēng yīn zhuā zhù lóng。
Wǒ men hái bù rú shì bǔ liǎo fēng,
dàn bù huì chéng rèn shī bài!

妈妈在厨房做饭,
奶奶站在旁边。
我們正准备迎新年,
是我全年最喜欢的一天!

" 我想我们好像缺少什么，"
我聽母亲說,
"一条龙会带来健康和幸运。"
一条龙!?什么??不可能!!

每年，朋友和我
帮助装饰街道。
每隔几英尺
我们挂一次飞春和红灯笼。

但这新的一年,
我们得观看有何线索。
哦，等一下，那是?我想我看到了……。
它是!一条真的红色龙的尾巴!

这条龙能控制水?
它比我们想象的要酷!
我们必须要更聪明。
才能把这条龙抓住!

我们不用玉米卷给这条龙——。
我们会试用面条和糯米饭。
问题是它很爱吃这些,
就回来吃了两次!

我以为我们的龙吃完,
它就想想午睡。
但是舒适龙客栈
也成不了陷阱!

我们希望现在能用
這雷鸣的声音抓住龙。
我們还不如是捕了风,
但不会承认失败!

We cannot lose this dragon now,
not with this massive bait!
A dragon can't resist some gold.
We'll catch him—just you wait!

On any other day, I'd love
to catch money from the sky.
But today it means our trap fell through…
I need just one more try!

This final trap just has to work.
It is our greatest chance!
The thing that dragons love the most?
The mighty Dragon Dance!

Our Dragon Dance is going great—
I'm having so much fun!
But where's our dragon? We've gotta catch him
before the day is done!

Oh man, we made a giant mess,
and no dragon to be seen.
That means no good health or fortune…
I guess we'd better clean.

"I'm sorry, Mom, I tried my best
to make you proud this year…"
Then she pulls me in a hug.
"I love this dragon best, right here."

Watching fireworks with Mom
and Grandma next to me,
I feel so lucky standing here
with my loving family.

Better luck next year!

Wǒ men xiàn zài bù néng shī qù zhè tiáo lóng,
shèn zhì yòng zhè me jù dà de yòu ěr!
Lóng wú fǎ kàng jù yī xiē huáng jīn。
Wǒ men huì zhuā zhù tā de——nǐ děng zhe ba!

Zài rèn hé tiān, wǒ zuì xǐ ài
cóng tiān shàng jiē zhù qián。
Dàn jīn tiān wǒ men de xiàn jǐng méi chéng gōng……
Wǒ xū yào zài shì yī cì!

Zhè zuì hòu de xiàn jǐng yào chéng gōng。
Zhè shì wǒ men zuì dà de jī huì!
Lóng zuì xǐ huan de dōng xī shì shén me?
Zhuàng dà de wǔ lóng!

Wǒ men wǔ lóng jìn xíng dé hǎo jí le——
Wǒ wán de hěn kāi xīn!
Dan wǒ men de lóng ne?
Jīn tiān jié shù qián yī dìng yào zhuā zhù tā!

Ó tiān na, wǒ men lòng dà zāo le!
Ér méi kàn dào lóng。
Nà yì si méi dài lái jiàn kāng yě méi fú qi le……
Wǒ xiǎng wǒ men zuì hǎo qīng lǐ gān jìng。

"Duì bu qǐ, mā ma, wǒ jìn lì le
Jīn nián xiǎng yào ràng nín jiāo ào……"
Rán hòu mā ma lā wǒ bào zhuó
"Wǒ zuì xǐ huan zhè tiáo lóng, jiù zài zhè lǐ。"

Hé mā ma, nǎi nai yī qǐ kàn yān huǒ,
Wǒ jué de hé wǒ qīn ài de jiā rén zhàn zài yī qǐ
shì rú cǐ de xìng yùn。

Zhù míng nián gèng hǎo yùn!

我们现在不能失去这条龙，
甚至用这么巨大的诱饵！
龙无法抗拒一些黄金。
我们会抓住它的——你等着吧！

在任何天，我最喜爱
从天上接住钱。
但今天我们的陷阱没成功……
我需要再试一次！

这最后的陷阱要成功。
这是我们最大的机会！
龙最喜欢的東西是什麼？
壮大的舞龙！

我们舞龙进行得好极了—-
我玩得很开心！
但我们的龙呢？
今天結束前一定要抓住它！

哦，天哪，我们弄大糟了！
而没看到龙。
那意思没带来健康也没福气了……
我想我们最好清理干净。

"对不起，妈妈，我尽力了
今年想要让您骄傲……"
然后妈妈拉我抱著。
"我最喜欢这条龙，就在这里。"

和妈妈，奶奶一起看烟火，
我觉得和我亲爱的家人站在一起
是如此的幸运。

祝明年更好运！

Copyright © 2019 by Sourcebooks
Text by Adam Wallace
Illustrations by Andy Elkerton
Cover and internal design © 2019 by Sourcebooks
Translation by Suk Lee

Sourcebooks and the colophon are registered trademarks of Sourcebooks, Inc.

The art was first sketched, then painted digitally with brushes designed by the artist.

Published by Sourcebooks Wonderland, an imprint of Sourcebooks Kids
P.O. Box 4410, Naperville, Illinois 60567-4410
(630) 961-3900
sourcebookskids.com

Library of Congress Cataloging-in-Publication Data is on file with the publisher.

Source of Production: 1010 Printing Asia Limited, North Point, Hong Kong, China
Date of Production: November 2022
Run Number: 5029234

Printed and bound in China.
OGP 10 9 8 7 6